MRS. OWL'S

TREATMENT PLAN FOR OCD

MRS. OWL'S

TREATMENT PLAN FOR OCD

CHRIS WIDDOP

Printed in the United States of America

Cover art by Christine Celenski
First Printing: 2025

ISBN 979-8-9876030-8-6

widdopc@velcrotheninjakat.com

www.VelcroTheNinjaKat.com

CONTENTS

THE WALLS ARE LAVA
5

JAY'S MONSTER
19

THE POISON FROG PRINCE
37

BIRDWATCHING
77

I suffer from a severe case of Obsessive Compulsive Disorder. Over the years, my OCD grew worse and worse, until I reached a point where it had essentially taken over every single aspect of my life, and felt inescapable. But I was able to get help, through a long journey of trial and error, and so my hope is to anyone who might be dealing with similar issues in their life to please don't give up, and seek the help you need as early as possible. It might take time, and it might be frustrating along the way, but for the sake of your life, you owe it to yourself to just keep moving forward.

My OCD is primarily based on

contamination, and navigating through life with this condition made me an absolutely miserable person. At my lowest, I was spending almost half of my waking hours doing what is referred to as "rituals", all in an attempt to keep my OCD at bay. But the more I gave in to these rituals, the more the OCD grew, until it became unbearable.

I was having near nightly panic attacks in response to my OCD. My nightly rituals of cleaning and washing myself typically lasted around six hours, and yet I'd still go to bed feeling dirty and gross. I knew that I needed help, and once my OCD reached a level where I literally couldn't work a full time job anymore due to the excessive time spent trying to quell it, I had to move back in to my mother's house and look into treatment options.

The first step I took involved looking into psychiatrists who could prescribe me with medication. I was a bit hesitant about doing this, as I had poor experiences in the past with medications prescribed to treat my depression and anxiety issues. And after giving the first medication a shot this time around, I was almost immediately feeling the same side effects that I had recalled feeling years before, and so I opted to look into alternative resources.

I looked up local therapists in town, and found one who listed OCD as one of the treatments they covered. So I went to my first therapist, who suggested we try EMDR (Eye Movement Desensitization and Reprocessing) treatment. I didn't really gel with this therapist though, and after my third appointment where it felt like she was intentionally dragging things out, I decided to stop seeing her. She understood, but was still able to recommend another program that more closely specialized in OCD treatment.

That program was at FSU, and their goal was to see my symptoms decline relatively quickly, through a combination of medication and exposure therapy. I was still hesitant about going the medication route, but I gave the exposure aspect a shot. We did see some improvement, but it was a very slow process, and after going to them for several months, my therapist eventually removed me from the program because I wasn't improving at a quick enough pace.

This was very disheartening, and for the next few months I wasn't entirely sure where to turn to next.

THE WALLS ARE LAVA

We've all heard of the children's game where we pretend the floor is lava, and we try to navigate around the room without stepping on it. Now imagine that, but it's not just the floor that's lava, but the walls around you as well. And imagine that it's not a game, but your personal purgatory that you have to experience every single night, a maze of lava and fire, and you don't get to stop playing until you've reached the end of the maze. That was Jay's reality.

Every night as Jay laid down in bed to go to sleep, once his eyes shut and he was drifting off into dreamland, he would suddenly seem to awaken in a fiery maze. It was a dark cave-like place, illuminated by sporadic flames. It took him hours of careful steps on the slabs of rocks that jutted up to avoid touching the lava on the floor or the walls that surrounded him. And there was something in his head that urged him to complete the maze. Not quite a voice, but something that spoke in images, pushing him forward and condemning him for making missteps along the way, even when he knew he hadn't made any mistakes.

At first, despite how real this experience felt, Jay figured that these were just a series of nightmares he had to endure every night. But once he would reach the end of the maze, he'd wake up back in bed in a puddle of sweat, and his arms appeared red from the overnight ordeal. The marks on Jay's arms got so bad that he decided to see a doctor about them. But upon telling his story, the doctor referred him to see a psychiatrist instead.

He booked an appointment with Mrs. Owl, who came recommended by the doctor, and he told her all about this horrific nightly routine of his.

"Why do you listen to this voice that speaks in pictures?" Mrs. Owl asked. "What would happen if you refused to do what it says?"

"It sets my brain on fire," said Jay. "And the only way to put it out is to start down the path and complete the maze again."

"I see. And what's at the end of this maze?" asked Mrs. Owl.

"That's just it, there's nothing there. It's a dead end, blocked off by a wall of lava. And it takes so long to get there that I'm completely exhausted. But if I close my eyes at that point, I'll find myself back in bed, but feeling sleep deprived as it's time for me to get up and start another day."

"And you feel as if these nightmares aren't really nightmares, but a reality for you?"

"How else would you explain the

burns on my arms?" asked Jay, showing off the redness of his skin.

"Have you ever touched the lava?" asked Mrs. Owl.

"No," Jay admitted. "I've tried before in the beginning, but the thing in my head set my brain aflame again, and wouldn't relent until I pulled back."

"If you haven't ever touched the lava, then how do you know that they're causing these marks on you?"

"What else could it be?" asked Jay.

"And you're sure that it's lava on the walls?" asked Mrs. Owl. "You feel its heat?"

"Well, that's the strange part. I don't," said Jay.

"So how do you know that it's real?" asked Mrs. Owl.

"Because of the burns," said Jay, who was growing frustrated at repeating himself.

"I see," said Mrs. Owl. "Have you ever thought about jumping into the lava?"

"I have," Jay admitted.

"What stops you?"

"I just can't bring myself to do it. I don't want it to end like this, and I can't let this thing in my head beat me."

"What if those marks on your arm aren't burns?" asked Mrs. Owl.

"What else could they be?" asked Jay.

"Perhaps that voice inside you is trying to take over. Each time you complete this nightly ritual, that thing grows stronger. And the stronger it grows, the more it consumes your body."

Jay looked down at his arms, and he considered what his psychiatrist was saying.

"You mean like I've been possessed by some sort of demon?" asked Jay. "But why? That doesn't make sense."

"None of this makes any sense," said Mrs. Owl. "And I theorize that it really is all in your head."

"But the marks..."

"I have some homework for you," Mrs. Owl interjected. "Tonight, I want you to touch the lava."

"But I can't..."

"I believe that you can," said Mrs. Owl. "And I believe that your way out of this purgatory is to confront this thing head on. No matter how badly it tries to burn you, I want you to power through it and touch the lava and see what happens. Can you do this?"

"I... I can try," Jay said sheepishly.

* * *

That night, Jay laid in his bed, and he closed his eyes to go to sleep. And after ahile, like every other night, he reopened his eyes to find himself once more in the maze of fire and lava. He wasted no time moving forward, cautiously stepping from stone to stone, contorting his body away from the lava walls as he moved down one hall and then to the next.

Minutes felt like hours. Hours felt like an eternity. And all the while, he was constantly being berated by the demon in his head, who threatened to set his head ablaze should he resist. The maze went on and on, and he was certain that it grew larger in scale each night. He always wondered if he would ever make it to the end, and sometimes he felt like he'd be trapped in this maze forever.

With sheer willpower and per-severance, he somehow managed to make it to the end of the maze. He was incredibly exhausted, his heart was racing, and he was breathing heavily, as tears of panic rolled down his cheeks. He was about to close his eyes, ready to wake up from the nightmare, when he remembered his homework assignment from Mrs. Owl.

He gulped, and then he lifted his hand to reach out. Immediately the demon set his brain on fire, inundating him with images of being burned alive. Jay wailed in agony, pleading for the demon to stop. He lowered his hand in submission to the demon's will, and he stared at the lava on the wall at the maze's dead end. He looked down at his arms, at their redness, and he stood still for a moment, trying to calm himself.

Gradually, the flames in his head subsided. Once the flames had completely dissipated, he focused on the wall of lava straight ahead, and he attempted again to accomplish the task at hand.

He took in a deep breath, bracing himself. Then, slowly, he reached out towards the wall once more. He could feel the fire beginning to return in his head, but he persisted, slowly bringing his hand closer to the lava. He winced, as his body twitched in resistance, but he pushed forward. His hand was mere inches from the lava, and he paused, as the fire inside his head raged even harder. He shook his head, then clenched his jaw, holding his breath as he hesitantly reached out with his index finger and lightly tapped the lava.

It was cold.

Confused, he then pressed his whole palm against the wall. As he did, he watched as the lava slid down from the wall and onto the floor, revealing a door that had been hidden behind it. Jay hesitated, and the demon raged. But he was able to endure the burning flames in his head, as he carefully brought his hand to the doorknob. Slowly he turned it. As the door creaked open, a light spilled into the maze from the other side. When Jay pushed the door fully open, he was blinded by the light that shined through.

He shielded his eyes, and as his vision adjusted, he gasped at the sight that lay on the other side of the door. The demon screamed inside of his head, and he winced at the pain that it caused him. But this time, he was able to shake off the pain and move past the flames, as he concentrated on the brilliant light shining on him.

Jay stepped through the door. And as a sense of relief fell over him, he closed the door behind him.

My mother did some research into alternative treatments, and she came across some articles that discussed the use of psilocybin mushrooms. The issue here was that these mushrooms weren't exactly something I could be prescribed or buy over the counter, so I wasn't really sure how to acquire them. I called up a few old friends from high school who I knew used to do that sort of thing back in the day, but none of them were able to help me out, as they had long stopped using the stuff.

However, one friend who I contacted mentioned how he was also dealing with symptoms of OCD, and his therapist had managed to work wonders in helping him get his life back on track. He gave me the information for his therapists office, and I reached out to schedule an appointment. This new therapist was finally a good match, and she genuinely wanted to help, and was willing to work with me at a pace that I was comfortable with, as well as respecting my wishes to not immediately jump into medication if we could avoid it.

I mentioned to her about what I had read about psilocybin, and though she wasn't sure where to acquire that, she suggested ketamine infusion treatments as a viable alternative. So I found a place in town, and I gave it a shot. The first treatment made me feel a great deal of relief afterwards, though that relief only lasted for a single day. Afterwards, my symptoms grew more intense, and that trend would continue to be the case after each infusion during my treatment trial.

JAY'S MONSTER

One frightful day a monster emerged from the ocean and threatened to destroy Jay's home city. Everyone ran for their lives as the monster knocked down buildings with ease, and it roared with dominance for all to hear.

Jay didn't run though. Instead, he met the monster head on, and manifested within himself a monster all his own. Jay was already a tall and lanky man, but as he transformed, his frame grew to colossal heights, and he confronted the opposing monster with new strength. The two monsters battled, but Jay's was able to overpower his opponent, and send him crawling back into the ocean defeated.

The citizens of the city stopped and cheered after Jay's miraculous victory over the sea monster. However, their sense of relief soon turned to horror, as Jay's monster continued to rampage through the city, toppling buildings and destroying everything it touched.

* * *

Sometime later, Jay managed to regain control from the monster, and he shrunk back down to his normal size. He looked around at the destruction he had wreaked on the city, and he fled in horror, lest his hidden monster reemerge and continue destroying the city he loved. But in the days and weeks to follow, every day the gargantuan beast within Jay would manifest itself and destroyed everything it touched.

Jay had completely lost control over the monster, and so one day, upon reverting back to his normal self, he finally sought help ridding himself of this terrible burden.

Jay visited the offices of Dr. Stein, and he explained his situation to the doctor, who pondered Jay's story with a look of uncertainty.

"Please, Dr. Stein, I need help," said Jay.

"There is a procedure we do here that could help suppress the monster," said Dr. Stein. He explained that the procedure would involve Jay being hooked up to a machine, which would then read his brainwaves and help realign his brain patterns so that he could gain control over himself. "We can try it, if you'd like."

"Yes, let's do it," said Jay.

Dr. Stein escorted Jay into a private room with a chair next to the machine, which had a myriad of wires. The doctor attached the machine's neural wires to Jay's head, then he left the room to let the machine do its work.

At first, Jay felt nothing out of the

ordinary. Then, all at once, his perception became incredibly distorted. His vision had blurred, and objects appeared to be stretching and swaying all around him. He felt completely out of control, and the experience left him feeling like a robot that was suddenly malfunctioning.

After the treatment had concluded, Jay needed help standing up out of the chair and exiting the room.

"How was it?" asked Dr. Stein.

"It was... weird," said Jay, still hazy from the procedure. He then explained his experience, and mentioned how he felt almost mechanical while he was under. "This monster in me, it wasn't created in a lab or something, was it?" Jay asked.

"Hmm," said Dr. Stein. "I'm not sure I have the answer to that."

Jay sighed in dismay. "Well how will I know if the treatment worked?"

"We won't know for sure until you've had a couple more treatments," said Dr.

Stein. "Hopefully you'll at least feel some relief though, and the monster won't reemerge in the meantime."

* * *

For a single day, Jay indeed felt relief.

Then the very next day, the monster returned with a vengeance, once again destroying everything it touched.

After the monster had expended itself and Jay returned to normal, he returned to Dr. Stein and expressed his concerns.

"The monster only grew stronger," Jay said. "It can't go on like this."

"I see," said Dr. Stein. "It's possible that the monster will grow stronger before it weakens. It's fighting for its survival, after all. I suggest we keep to the program for now."

With a feeling of unease, Jay agreed to move forward with the second treatment. Dr. Stein hooked him back up to the machine, then he left the room to let the machine do its work.

Where as before he felt like a robot gone haywire, this time the treatment pushed him even further, to where he felt like he had been transported to a dreamlike state, one that was inescapable.

After the treatment had concluded, the dreaminess gradually subsided, and Dr. Stein entered the room to help him out of the chair again.

"How was it?" asked Dr. Stein.

"I felt like I was stuck in a dream," Jay said.

"Well you're unstuck now, so now we wait and see how your body takes it. Hopefully you'll feel a little relief, and the monster will be quieted for a while."

* * *

There was no period of relief.

The monster returned with a fury, and

resumed destroying everything it touched.

After the monster had exerted itself again, Jay returned to Dr. Stein to once again express his concerns.

"The monster grew even stronger this time," Jay said.

"I see," said Dr. Stein. "Well, we only have one more treatment left before we'll know for sure if this procedure will work for you, and I'd suggest we give it one last chance."

With a feeling of unease, Jay reluctantly agreed to move forward with the final treatment. Dr. Stein hooked him back up to the machine, then he left the room to let the machine do its work.

Jay's perception grew distorted, and he entered the dreamlike state again. But this time, the treatment pushed him even further than before, to the point where Jay felt as if he was about to black out. He felt like an astronaut being launched into space, and he was holding on for dear life to not entirely lose his senses.

After the treatment had concluded, this near blackout experience gradually faded away, and Dr. Stein entered the room to help him out of the chair one last time.

"How was it?" asked Dr. Stein.

"It was... *intense*," Jay said.

"That's good," said Dr. Stein. "That's normal."

"So what now?" asked Jay.

"Now we see if this treatment will work for you," said Dr. Stein. "But if the monster reemerges again, I'm afraid to say that this might not be the solution for you."

* * *

The monster reemerged.

It was even more powerful this time, and it raged through the city, destroying everything in its way.

After the monster had exerted itself again, Jay returned to Dr. Stein to see what else could be done.

"I'm not sure I have the answer to that," said Dr. Stein.

"If you don't, then who would?" asked Jay.

Dr. Stein had recommended another specialist who might be able to help him, and Jay visited the offices of Mrs. Owl. He explained his situation to her, and she pondered Jay's story with genuine curiosity.

"Please, Mrs. Owl, I need help," said Jay.

"I hear your concerns," said Mrs. Owl, "but I want you to consider the following. You talk about this monster like it's a different being within you. But the truth is, the monster *is* you," she said. "Or at least, it's a part of you."

"But how do I get rid of it then?" asked Jay.

"That's impossible," said Mrs. Owl. "However, what *is* possible is that we can weaken it, so that you can regain control of yourself and overpower it."

"But how will we do that?" asked Jay. "The last treatment program only made the monster grow stronger."

"Each treatment works differently for everyone," Mrs. Owl explained, "and we were able to rule this procedure out for you. So that just means we need to move onto the next option."

Jay hesitated with his response. "But what if the next one doesn't work either? What if it also makes the monster stronger?"

"Then we'll continue onto the next option, and then the next, and then the next, until we finally do find what works for you. Are you willing to do that?"

Jay was uncertain, but he seriously considered the plan she proposed.

"Okay," Jay finally said. "Yes, let's do it."

After ketamine didn't work out, my therapist recommended I look into marijuana, and told me about a place in town where it could be purchased legally. I went there and bought a gummy, and they recommended that I only take half of it, and I did so over the next two days. It gave me a lightheaded sensation, but didn't actually give me any relief of my symptoms, so that quickly got ruled out as well.

Shortly afterward, I reached out to some other friends, and I finally found one who was able to hook me up with psilocybin. The first two times I took it, I took what is referred to as a microdose, but like the marijuana, all this really did was make me feel lightheaded, and it didn't really improve my symptoms. The third time I tried it, I took a much larger dose, and I was able to fully feel the trippy effects. I came away understanding how this substance could certainly be helpful for some, but for me, it still offered me no relief even at a higher dose.

I reported my findings back to my therapist, and during this time, we were undergoing a combination of EMDR treatment, as well as exposure therapy, which was having slow results like before. Also during this time I continued to look into other potential treatments, and followed through on an appointment for neurofeedback at the suggestion of someone at work, but that, too, didn't help my cause. My therapist also suggested looking into inpatient treatment, but after looking up treatment centers all across the globe, my conclusion was that such centers are clearly only made to help treat millionaires who are suffering, as the prices were far out of my reach.

The next thing I looked into was transcranial magnetic stimulation therapy, where they treat your brain with the use of magnets. This was also a very expensive procedure, and by this point, I wasn't confident that the results would look any different from anything else I had already tried out. So, with all other options exhausted, my therapist finally insisted that I try giving medication another shot.

She recommended Prozac, which is a medication that was supposed to be especially helpful for people suffering from OCD. So I looked up my psychiatrist at the local hospital again, and they recommended I turn to the Neighborhood Medical Center. There, before seeing the psychiatrist, they wanted to check on my general health, and discovered that there were issues with my thyroid. They prescribed thyroid medication for the condition, which in addition to treatment my thyroid, also helped in improving my mood in general, though I was still suffering from my OCD.

I was finally able to see my psychiatrist at this point, and I went over my history of treatments, as well as my history of medication, and mentioned the Prozac recommendation from my therapist. So he prescribed it to me, and initially, it did make me feel worse. However, my therapist assured me that that could be a good sign, that it'll get worse before it gets better, and urged me to stick to it. And after about a week or so, I did finally see improvements.

Now that I was on medication, my therapist wanted us to move on to more intense exposure therapy. I was able to follow through on what was asked of me, and I was able to do so without my OCD bothering me like it would have in the past. My psychiatrist gradually increased my Prozac dose to the maximum, and then started adding Abilify to augment its effects. And through the use of these medications, as well as sticking to my therapy, I was finally able to get my life back on track.

THE POISON FROG PRINCE

I

Once upon a time, there was a prince named Jay. One sunny day Prince Jay was practicing his sword skills in the castle's training grounds, parrying with his loyal advisor and trusted combat instructor Henry.

"Tonight is the night, Henry," said Prince Jay with a swipe.

"The night for what?" asked Henry, evading the strike. "That you best me in swordsmanship? I think not!"

Henry swiped back, but Prince Jay blocked the blow with his blade.

"No no, not that. Tonight, I intend to

ask the lovely Princess Valerie for her hand, and to join our two houses in marriage."

"Well that's wonderful news indeed," said Henry. "I do hope it goes well."

Prince Jay then struck at Henry's hilt, and he succeeded in disarming his dance partner.

"I'd say things are going my way so far," said the prince with a smirk.

"Touché," said Henry.

Prince Jay knelt down to retrieve Henry's sword, then handed it back to his advisor.

"I see you've learned well in the way of swordplay," said Henry. "But before your night's quest, may I suggest you go over your plan with me, and we'll see if you need a lesson on the ways to a woman's heart."

The two sheathed their swords with a shared laugh, and they trotted away from the training grounds to prepare for the evening's affairs. But unbeknownst to them, their private conversation had been overheard by another, as a young man named Julian peeked from around a corner and watched them recede, with a jealous scorn on his face.

Julian continued to follow them silently, keeping out of sight. Once they reached Prince Jay's quarters, Henry departed to give the prince a chance to change his clothes and clean himself up. With Henry out of the way, the young man made his move. He rapped at the door to the prince's quarters, then stepped back to distance himself.

"I told you to give me a minute," Prince Jay spoke brusquely, but once he opened the door a look of confusion came over his face. "Oh, you're not Henry."

"I'm afraid not," said Julian. "And I'm afraid that Princess Valerie shall not be accepting your proposal tonight, either."

"I beg your pardon?" asked Prince Jay with a tone of disbelief at the audacity of the young man.

Julian then raised his hands in a threatening manner.

"You dare raise your hands at me?" demanded Prince Jay.

"Oh, I dare more than that," said Julian. He waved his hands through the air, casting a spell over the prince, for it turned out that this was no ordinary young man, but in fact a sorcerer.

Prince Jay was stunned, and he rapidly began to shrink in size, sinking down into his clothes.

"I always did advise my king that it was trouble coming to these lands," said the sorcerer ominously. "Too bad for you he didn't listen to me, but now with you out of the way, there's nobody else standing between me and my bride to be, Princess Valerie."

"What have you done to me?" demanded the prince.

"Why, I've turned you into a frog," said Julian with glee. "And what princess would want to marry such a creature?"

Julian then put on a pair of gloves, and with the snap of his fingers he conjured a small cage out of thin air. He cautiously stepped towards the prince, then leaned down and wrapped his gloved hand around the frog's body.

"Unhand me, you fiend!" Prince Jay commanded.

"As you wish," said Julian, and he dropped the prince into the cage. He locked it shut, and placed it on the floor of the prince's quarters. "Now if you'll excuse me, tonight is the night in which *I* intend to ask the lovely Princess Valerie for her hand in marriage." The sorcerer laughed, and he closed Prince Jay in his room.

* * *

The prince spent the afternoon trying to escape from the cage. He tugged at the lock, and tried to pry the bars open, but nothing would budge.

As the day wore on, his stomach rumbled with hunger. He heard a fly zipping about, and instinctively he darted his tongue at it and swallowed the bug. The prince gagged, disgusted by his own actions, but after a lick of his lips, an idea sprang to mind.

The prince scanned the room until his eyes landed on his sword, which was still in its sheath. He hurled his tongue out at the sword's hilt and managed to latch on. Bracing himself, the prince then snapped his tongue back into his mouth, and in doing so he was able to snatch the sword from its sheath and send it hurling towards the cage, where the blade sliced through the bars.

Finally free, the prince hopped out of the cage, and he went to retrieve his sword. However, with his small stature he found it far too clumsy to handle the sword, and he figured he'd be useless with it in combat while in his current state. "Well this just won't do," he said with disappointment.

He dropped the sword and wracked his brain for solutions. He looked around the room again, and from his low vantage point on the ground he saw an old chest he had stored away under his bed.

"Ah! I know just the thing," he said, and he hopped over to the chest. He tugged at the chest, dragging it from under the bed, and then he quickly popped it open. He rummaged around through his old knick-knacks until he found what he was looking for, and he snatched up an old toy soldier.

"I think this should work," he said, relieving the toy soldier of its sword. He swung his new sword out and jabbed at the air. "Perfect!"

It was late, and Prince Jay figured that Julian would be making his way to Princess Valerie soon. So with his sword in hand, he rushed out of the room, and he hopped over to the guest quarters where the princess was staying. The prince was just in time, and as he approached he saw the young sorcerer nearing the princess' room, formally dressed and with a bouquet of flowers in hand.

"You there!" the prince shouted, startling Julian. "Face me this instant, I command you!"

Julian was unimpressed by the sight of the frog prince, and he chuckled as his flowers suddenly changed form into a sword with the wave of his hand.

"Very well, let's make this quick," said the sorcerer.

The two engaged in combat, and as their swords clashed the prince found himself much more agile as a frog. It wasn't long before the more experienced prince had bested his adversary, disarming the young sorcerer and toppling him onto his back.

Prince Jay pressed his blade against the throat of his opponent, and at that same moment the door to Princess Valerie's room swung open.

"What's all this commotion about?" asked the princess, who was shocked by the scene outside her door.

"As you can see, my dear, this sorcerer of yours has transformed me into a frog."

The princess was confused by the talking frog. "Jay? Is that really you?"

"It is indeed," confirmed Prince Jay.

"And is this true that you did this to the prince, Julian?" Valerie asked the sorcerer.

"It is not," Julian said initially, until the prince pressed harder against his throat. "Okay, it is."

"How could you?" the princess gasped.

"Now, I command you to reverse the spell this instant," said Prince Jay.

A smile formed on Julian's face in response.

"What are you smiling about?"

"That's just it, *I* can't reverse this spell. It can only be broken in one manner."

The prince narrowed his eyes. "And what manner would that be?"

"This spell can only be broken by a kiss from one's true love," laughed the sorcerer. "And as I said before, who could love such a creature as you?"

The prince lowered his blade, and he took a deep breath. "Well, this isn't the manner that I had hoped to do this, but..."

Prince Jay turned to the princess, and he hopped up to her. "Princess Valerie, truly you are the love of my life. Would you do me the honor of being my wife?"

"Oh, Jay." Valerie's eyes filled with tears of joy. "Of course I'll marry you."

She knelt down and placed her hands on the ground for the prince, and he hopped into her palms. Brimming with joy, she slowly raised her hands towards her face. The princess closed her eyes, and the prince did as well, as he puckered his frog lips.

However, before their lips could touch, her hands froze in place. Prince Jay opened his eyes, and he saw that the princess appeared to go stiff.

"Valerie? Is everything alright?"

Her jaw gaped open, and her eyes sprang wide in fright. She dropped the prince, and he tumbled back to the ground.

"What's happening? Valerie, what's wrong?"

Princess Valerie couldn't speak though, for her voice was caught in her throat.

"*Fool*," Julian laughed, "I didn't turn you into just *any* type of frog, but one who is poisonous to the touch!"

Prince Jay gasped as he watched his betrothed fall to the ground, and he watched the life slowly slip from her eyes.

"But why?" asked the prince. "Why would you do this? I thought you loved her, too."

"Oh, I do," said Julian. "But if I can't have her, then *no one* can."

"You *monster.*"

The prince raised his sword again, and he charged at the sorcerer. But before the prince could strike him down, a burst of smoke enveloped him. When the smoke cleared, Julian had vanished from sight.

Suddenly all alone, the sword slipped from the prince's grasp, clanking as it hit the ground. He turned to face the body of his beloved Princess Valerie laying on the ground, and his shoulders slumped in defeat.

II

After the tragedy with Princess Valerie, Prince Jay locked himself in isolation within his quarters. There he stayed for days, and then weeks at a time, surviving off of the sporadic bugs that managed to crawl inside. Every day, Henry would come to the prince's door to knock and check in on him. But every day, the prince would turn Henry away.

This day looked to be no different, as Henry once more dutifully came to check on the prince.

"Leave me," said the prince.

This time, however, Henry responded,

"No, I think I won't do that."

"Pardon me?" Prince Jay asked, surprised by the blatant disregard for his wishes.

"Prince Jay, enough time has passed. You can't stay locked in your room forever. How are you to rule this kingdom one day if you won't even step outside and look upon it?"

The prince sighed in frustration. "Don't you understand it's not that simple? I can't touch anybody, lest they fall to their demise. It's not safe. And besides, after what I did to Valerie..."

"Let me stop you right there. That was *not* your fault, and I refuse to allow you to go on believing that it was. You didn't choose to be transformed into a frog, and you certainly had no way of knowing that you were poisonous. That blame falls squarely upon that wretched sorcerer Julian."

"That's easy enough to say," said the

prince, "but you weren't the one who did it."

Henry sighed with understanding. "That may be so, but still, you have to forgive yourself. You owe it not just to yourself, but to Princess Valerie as well, to keep moving forward."

"But what is there to move forward to, Henry? I'm stuck this way now."

"Well what if there was another way to break the spell?" asked Henry.

"Do you know of another way?"

"No, I do not. *But*, I do know of a place where you could perhaps find the answers that you're seeking."

Prince Jay paused and then said to his loyal advisor, "Wait just a moment." He hopped off the bed and once more tugged the chest out, and opened it up to retrieve the toy soldier. He pulled off the soldier's gloves, slipping them over his webbed hands. He hopped over to the door, and for the first time in what felt like forever, he jumped up to unlock the latch and the door creaked as he cautiously opened it.

"Tell me what you know, Henry."

"There's a forest. A Forest of Visions. It's a place where those who are lost go to wander and find themselves."

"A Forest of Visions?" asked the prince. "And how is it that you know of this place?"

"I wouldn't be a very good advisor if I wasn't familiar with such places, now would I?" Henry responded with a wink.

"Fair enough," Prince Jay said, nodding. "A Forest of Visions, hmm... Okay, I'm willing to give it a shot. Henry, tell me how to get to this forest."

* * *

His sword at his side and his gloves on his hands, Prince Jay traveled to the place that Henry had told him about. As he hopped into the forest, there didn't initially appear to be anything out of the ordinary. He continued down the path as he trekked deeper, hearing birds singing and squirrels scrambling up trees, and seeing the occasional deer frolicking about.

Soon though, the forest began to change. He noticed the trees around him started swaying and stretching, almost like they were dancing, despite the calm air. And as he glanced around, it was as if he could see more clearly than ever before. Even the usual blur from the turning of his head had seemingly vanished, as his world became crystal clear in that moment. The prince was wowed by the experience, and couldn't stop from admiring the beauty of the forest around him. As he traveled even deeper within, the trees appeared to have a glow to them.

"What sort of place is this?" the prince wondered aloud.

But then, as the prince entered a clearing, all at once the world around him went dark, and the noises of nature went quiet. All he could hear was what sounded like a musical instrument of some sort being distorted, a sound that disturbed him and sent a chill through his body.

When the prince looked around in the darkness for the source of the noise, he heard a voice whisper, "You should not be here."

"Who are you?" demanded the prince. "Reveal yourself."

"I am you," said the voice.

"*What?* You are me? What is that supposed to mean?"

"I am the poison that resides within you," said the voice.

"The *poison?*" The prince glared with anger at the revelation. "What do you want? Have you not taken enough from me already?"

"No."

"*No?* You took Valerie from me, and you kill everything that you touch. How is that not enough?"

The poison didn't respond.

"Well, if you claim to be me, then surely you must do as I command," said the prince.

"No."

"But you're killing people. And you're killing me as well in the process."

"So be it," said the poison. "I am a part of you now. A part that has always been there in some form. And there is no getting rid of me."

"What is it that you want?" asked the prince.

"To be," said the poison.

The prince scoffed. "To be? And is that not what those who you touch also want, don't you think?"

"I don't care."

"Clearly I can see that," the prince seethed. "No, you are *not* me. I refuse to believe that. You are a demon who has attached itself to me."

"Believe what you will," the poison said with nonchalance.

The sound of a frog's ribbit snapped Prince Jay out of his trance. Suddenly he was back in the clearing, and the sights and sounds of the forest had returned, replacing the darkness and the disturbing distorted noises. On the other end of the clearing, the prince could see another frog had appeared, and was hopping his way.

The prince hopped towards the frog, meeting him in the middle of the clearing. "Hello, my good, er, frog?" the prince said.

The frog just stared blankly at the prince, and let out another ribbit.

"I see..." said the prince, unsure what to make of this new companion.

The frog then opened its mouth. It unraveled its tongue, and it dropped a vial on the ground before the prince. As Prince Jay retrieved the vial, the frog's tongue snapped back into its mouth, and the prince inspected the object in his gloved hands.

"Is this what I've come here in search of?" asked the prince.

But once more, the frog merely ribbited in response and turned and hopped away, leaving Prince Jay to ponder about the mysterious vial and all that he had encountered in this Forest of Visions.

III

Prince Jay reported back to Henry about his experiences in the Forest of Visions. He handed the vial to Henry, who inspected it carefully.

"So you spoke to the poison, and then the forest presented you with this vial in response. Perhaps this is an antidote of some sort," mused Henry. "I'm curious if you're meant to take this, so as to dilute the poison within you."

"But what if it kills me?" asked Prince Jay.

"I suppose that's a possibility," said Henry. "But if that were the case, then why would the forest give it to you?"

Prince Jay deliberated over this hypothesis, but he still wasn't entirely convinced. Finally, he said, "If there's a possibility this substance could rid me of the poison, then I suppose it's worth a try."

"I'm glad to hear it," said Henry. "In that case, while you were away, I decided to look into specialists on such matters, and I took the liberty of inviting a guest to the castle to aid with your treatment, someone with a far better knowledge in this field than I. Might I introduce you to Mrs. Owl."

Henry stepped aside so that Mrs. Owl could enter the room, and he made his leave with a bow.

"A pleasure to meet you, Your Highness," said Mrs. Owl.

"A pleasure?" asked Prince Jay. "Hmm, I suppose we'll see."

With Mrs. Owl's aid, the prince took a dose of the substance. Immediately after consuming it he grabbed at his head in agony.

"What's wrong?" asked Mrs. Owl in fright.

The distorted musical sounds had returned to his ears, and Prince Jay cried out, "It feels like my head is on *fire*." He endured the shuddering sensation though, and then after a moment he was able to shake off the feeling. Soon the screaming in his head had dissipated as well. "Okay, how do we know if this antidote worked?"

"Well I'd say to make sure, now you have to touch someone," said Mrs. Owl. "We should perhaps start with something smaller. How about one of those bugs that you're so fond of dining on?"

"Hmm," the prince pondered, as his eyes scanned the room. Upon seeing a fly zipping about, he instinctively latched onto it with his long tongue, swallowing the bug whole without a second thought.

"*Okay*," said Mrs. Owl. "Next time, perhaps let's not *eat* the bug before seeing if it survives your touch."

* * *

Each day Prince Jay tried touching the bugs. And each day they continued to die at his touch. The prince was growing increasingly disconcerted, just as the burning screams in his head continued to haunt him with every passing day.

"The process takes time," Mrs. Owl assured, and urged the prince to stick with his routine. Begrudgingly the prince placed faith in his counselor's confidence and continued the routine, taking another dose from the vial each day, and touching the bugs he would find to see if he still had a poison touch.

Then one day, with all hope gone, a fly landed on the prince's head. He didn't appear to be the least bit concerned with it though, and waited for it to die so that he could have his afternoon snack. However, after a moment's rest, the fly flew off, and floated away to safety.

The prince watched, waiting for the fly to drop. But it didn't.

"Did you just see that?"

"I did indeed," said Mrs. Owl. "I think the antidote is finally starting to work."

"Well that's great news," said Prince Jay, elated.

"And now that we've seen a fly survive, I think we should see what else can."

* * *

With his gloves on his hands, Prince Jay ventured outdoors with Mrs. Owl to the neighboring woods in the kingdom. They wandered around to see what creatures might be scurrying about, when a squirrel caught their attention.

Prince Jay slowly approached it, but

stopped when he heard Mrs. Owl clearing her throat. "The gloves," she reminded.

The prince looked at his hands, and reluctantly he removed his gloves. Cautiously he hopped over to the squirrel, and he began to reach out to it, but he hesitated.

"It'll be alright," Mrs. Owl encouraged him.

With a gulp, he pressed his palm down on the squirrel's head. He grimaced at the touch, holding his breath as he looked at the squirrel with concern. But the squirrel merely blinked in confusion. It shook his hand off and rushed up a tree's trunk, and Prince Jay sighed with relief as he watched it scurry away.

"I wonder though," said Prince Jay, "has my poison truly been treated?"

"What do you mean?" asked Mrs. Owl.

"Perhaps they're still doomed, but now there's merely a delayed response compared to before."

"Hmm," wondered Mrs. Owl. "Why don't we keep watching this squirrel, and see what happens."

And so they did just that, following the squirrel through the afternoon, watching it move about in good health.

"Well considering that before everyone that you touched fell instantly to the poison, I'd say that I feel good by the results that we're seeing thus far," said Mrs. Owl.

"Maybe," said the prince. "But I'm only touching these creatures briefly. If I continue to hold on to them, will my poison eventually seep out?"

A deer happened to cross their path at that point, and Mrs. Owl urged, "Why don't we put that theory to test? Go ahead and hop on that deer's back, ride it around for a little bit, and let's see what happens." Prince Jay appeared hesitant to do as suggested, but Mrs. Owl encouraged him, "You can do this."

With a gulp, the prince hopped over

to the deer. The deer bowed its head in greeting, then knelt down to let the prince hop onto its back. The deer stood up, and slowly, Prince Jay pressed down with his hands on the deer's back, grabbing two handfuls of fur. He rode on the deer as it strolled around the woods, and the longer he rode, the more the prince's worries slipped away like a cool breeze.

After some time Prince Jay hopped off.

"And now we watch and see what happens," said Mrs. Owl.

The deer turned to wander off, but it stumbled in its step. Prince Jay's breath caught in his chest. But the deer quickly recovered, shaking it off, and it glanced over at Prince Jay with a nod of farewell before prancing away into the woods.

"He looked pretty healthy to me," said Mrs. Owl.

"Yes, yes he did," said Prince Jay, and he stared down at his hands, marveling. "So the antidote really did work after all."

"I wouldn't get too excited just yet," cautioned Mrs. Owl.

"What do you mean?"

"We still have one last thing to test."

"What's that?" asked the prince.

Mrs. Owl then dropped to her knees. She cupped her hands together, then lowered them down to Prince Jay, gesturing for him to hop in for this final test.

"No, I can't," said the prince. "The risk is still too great."

"But you must," insisted Mrs. Owl.

The prince averted his gaze, unable to look Mrs. Owl in the eyes.

"It's okay," said Mrs. Owl, "you can do this. I know that you can. And I know that I'll be okay, too."

"Mrs. Owl..."

"Just take your time. I'll still be here when you're ready."

Guardedly, Prince Jay hopped over to Mrs. Owl. Carefully he reached out with a single finger. He winced as he moved it slowly forward little by little, until finally, he had made contact with Mrs. Owl's hands. The prince glanced up to ensure that Mrs. Owl was alright, and Mrs. Owl nodded her head. The prince nodded back, then taking a deep breath, he hopped into Mrs. Owl's palms, still terrified by the prospect that he may have just doomed her.

"I knew you could do it," said Mrs. Owl, who appeared unharmed.

"So I really am cured then, aren't I?" asked the prince.

"I'm not sure that 'cured' would be the correct term," said Mrs. Owl. "There's still the possibility that the poison could return should you cease taking the antidote."

"But there's only so much of the antidote left," said the prince. "Are you saying that the poison will return after I've run out?"

"I wouldn't worry about that just yet," Mrs. Owl said with a wink. "First, I think we should focus on breaking this spell."

IV

Prince Jay traveled to Princess Valerie's home kingdom. He entered the chapel and hopped over to the glass casket where her body was carefully laid.

"Oh, Valerie," he said, still in a state of disbelief at the sight of her corpse.

"All that work for nothing," he then heard the whisper in his head again, and the distorted musical instruments began to play as the poison spoke to him. "I have already taken your true love. So once that antidote runs out, you will be stuck with me for good, and then there will be nothing you can do to stop me."

"Quiet, you," said the prince, and he pulled out the vial. He took his daily dose of the antidote, and he listened as the noises in his head began to fade.

The prince then opened the glass case, and he looked down upon Princess Valerie. Tears began to well up in his eyes at the sight of her, and he leaned down to softly kissed her on the lips.

He turned and hopped away, unable to bear the sight of her lifeless body any longer, but then he heard something mo-]ving behind him.

"What's this? Where am I?" he heard a woman's voice speak.

Prince Jay turned in amazement as Princess Valerie sat up in her casket, looking tired and confused.

"Oh, Valerie!" Prince Jay wailed, hopping with joy at the sight of her.

"What's going on?" asked Princess Valerie. "What's happened?"

"I'm not sure," said the prince. "Perhaps the antidote that I just took was still on my lips when I kissed you just now. And perhaps it worked its magic and destroyed the poison within you, and brought you back to life."

"Oh, Jay," Princess Valerie said, as happy tears began streaming down her face.

He hopped back over to her, and she quickly scooped him up into her hands. She lifted the prince to her face, and she planted a passionate kiss on his frog lips. Immediately Prince Jay began to transform, growing rapidly in size until he was once more a fully grown man.

With the biggest smiles on their faces, Prince Jay and Princess Valerie looked lovingly into each others eyes. And they lived happily ever after.

I was now in a place where I was able to address other issues that had been holding me back in life as well, and which my therapist had theorized was related to OCD. I also suffer from selective mutism, where I have trouble speaking around members of my family. It's a condition that started later in life for me, and certainly worsened over the years, not unlike my experience with OCD. And my therapist suggested that my mutism was perhaps an extension of my OCD, where it was viewing my relationships with my family as yet another contamination to be avoided, and it did so by withdrawing to such an extreme degree that I found it difficult to even speak around them. And so, this became our next obstacle to tackle.

BIRDWATCHING

Part I

Blue Jay was going about his day, flying from branch to branch and whistling to the beat of his song. As he flew through the woods on his way back home, he crossed paths with a squirrel.

"Hello, Mr. Squirrel," sang Jay.

"Hello, Mr. Jay," said the squirrel.

Next on his path home, he flew past a rather large bush, and he happened upon a deer on the other side.

"Hello, Mr. Deer," sang Jay.

"Hello, Mr. Jay," said the deer.

Then he arrived at the tree where his home was. He landed on a branch, then he felt as his body tightened up. He took a deep breath, then he entered his home within the tree.

"Hello, Jay," sang Mother Jay.

But Blue Jay didn't sing anything back.

"How was your day today?" asked Mother Jay.

Blue Jay shrugged his shoulders, and he looked away.

He retreated into his room, and he could hear his mother sigh. As he closed the door, he let out a sigh of his own, and he was able to loosen up a bit once more.

> > >

The next day, as Blue Jay was about to leave home, Mother Jay stopped him on his way out.

"Good bye, Jay," she sang. "Have a good day."

But Blue Jay didn't sing anything

back.

He nodded his head and gave her a small smile, then he promptly flew out into the woods.

The further he flew, the more his body relaxed. And soon, he was able to sing again, though on this day, his song sounded rather sorrowful.

"Hello, Mr. Jay," he heard an owl hoot at him.

He hadn't even noticed her there on the tree branch, and was startled by the greeting.

"Oh, hello, Mrs. Owl," sang Jay.

"What's wrong, dear?" asked Mrs. Owl. "You don't seem your usual self today, and your song sounds so sad."

"I suppose it's because I *am* sad," said Jay. "I can sing all day long, but as soon as I return home, I lose my song."

"Well why do you suppose that is, dear?" asked Mrs. Owl.

"I don't know, I suppose I just feel

uncomfortable at home."

"Well what makes you feel uncomfortable at home?" asked Mrs. Owl.

"I don't know, I suppose I just feel uncomfortable when I'm around Mother Jay."

"Well what makes you feel uncomfortable around Mother Jay?" asked Mrs. Owl.

"I used to know," said Jay. "But I suppose I don't anymore. It's been so long since I've been able to sing around her, that I don't know how to bring myself to do it anymore."

"You're able to sing around me, though, right?" asked Mrs. Owl.

"Well, yes, I suppose that's right," said Jay.

"Well why not try bringing Mother Jay with you, and let's see if I can't help you sing around her, too?"

"Oh no, I couldn't do that," said Jay. "I'd be much too scared, and much too abashed."

"Well think about it," said Mrs. Owl, and she wished him well and went on her way.

>>>

That night, Blue Jay returned home and, just like before, his body tightened up. He took a deep breath, then he entered his home within the tree.

"Hello, Jay," sang Mother Jay.

But Blue Jay didn't sing anything back.

"How was your day today?" asked Mother Jay.

Blue Jay shrugged his shoulders, and he looked away.

"Oh, how I miss your voice," Mother Jay lamented. "I do wish you'd sing to me again someday."

Blue Jay's heart pounded, and he retreated into his room. He could hear his mother sigh again, and he let out a sigh of his own as he closed the door behind him. After calming down, he was able to lighten up a bit once more.

>>>

The next day, Blue Jay left his home and sought out Mrs. Owl.

"Hello, Mrs. Owl," sang Jay.

"Hello, Jay," said Mrs. Owl. "What brings you here today?"

"I've reconsidered your offer," said Jay. "I've decided that I can't bear the discomfort at home anymore."

"Well that's good to hear," said Mrs. Owl. "Just bring your mother with you the next time you seek me, and I'll be happy to help."

"But how can I get her to join me if I can't bring myself to sing around her?" asked Jay.

"Hmm," Mrs. Owl thought for a moment. "Perhaps I can join you then, and I can help you out at home."

"Oh no, I couldn't do that," said Jay. "I'd be much too scared, and much too abashed."

"Well think about it," said Mrs. Owl, and she wished him well and went on her way.

> > >

That night, Blue Jay returned home and, yet again, his body tightened up. He took a deep breath, then he entered his home within the tree.

"Hello, Jay," sang Mother Jay.

But Blue Jay didn't sing anything back.

He waited for his mother to ask about his day, but she didn't. So he retreated into his room. He could hear his mother sigh. As he closed the door behind him, he let out a sigh of his own, but this time he wasn't able to loosen back up, and instead his breathing grew heavy, and his heart started pounding again.

>>>

The next day, Blue Jay left his home and sought out Mrs. Owl once more.

"Hello, Mrs. Owl," sang Jay.

"Hello, Jay," said Mrs. Owl. "What brings you here today?"

"I've once again reconsidered your offer," said Jay. "I've decided that it would be okay for you to join me at home."

"Well that's good to hear," said Mrs. Owl. "Lead the way."

And so Blue Jay led Mrs. Owl back to his home. Upon arrival, his body tightened up, and he took a deep breath. He then entered his home within the tree.

"Hello, Jay," said Mother Jay. "Oh, who's this with you?"

"Hello, Mother Jay, I'm Mrs. Owl."

"Pleased to meet you," said Mother

Jay. "What brings you here today?"

"I was hoping to see if I could help Blue Jay here be able to sing around you again," said Mrs. Owl.

"Oh, that would be *wonderful*," exclaimed Mother Jay.

Mother Jay escorted Mrs. Owl into their living room, where all three birds perched on a seat. Mrs. Owl then began explaining what she had in mind to Mother Jay, but as she spoke, Blue Jay's mind retreated, and so too did his eyes. Soon, he found himself glancing out the window, watching the other birds outside.

* * *

"Jay," he heard his name.

Immediately, Jay was snapped back into reality. And in reality, he wasn't a bird at all, but a young man, sitting within his living room and looking out the window, daydreaming as he watched the birds flying around and singing outside.

"Jay," his name was repeated, and the man turned to face his therapist, Mrs. Owl, who was seated in the living room along with his mother. "Are you still with us, Jay?"

Jay nodded his head.

"It's okay, we're not birds. You don't have to sing," said Mrs. Jay. "I just want you to say '*hello*'."

Jay sat there hesitantly. He looked at his mother, and then he averted his gaze. His body tightened, and he took a deep breath. Then he opened his mouth to speak.

Part II

Jay always had a song in his head, at least when the frequency came through clear.

After much hard work, he was finally able to say "hello" to his mother, and then gradually he was able to speak to her as well. The more he spoke, the easier it got, and the more the radio waves in his head became less staticky within his mother's vicinity.

One session, Mrs. Owl asked Jay why he supposes it is that he behaves differently around different people or situations. Jay pondered over this question, then he turned his head and looked out the window, where he could just make out the sounds of singing birds.

* * *

After the session with Mrs. Owl, Blue Jay spread his wings and ventured outside to join his singing friends. At first their song sounded a bit off, like it was barely coming through. But after adjusting the radio knob in his head, he was able to find a clear channel, and he joined the other birds in singing along to the communal upbeat tune.

Jay then heard someone clearing their throat behind him, which made the channel go fuzzy again. When he turned around he found the source of the interference, which turned out to be the Boss Bird, who was standing over him with a glaring expression.

"What do you think you're all doing?" said the Boss Bird. "This is no time for play.

Get back to work, we've got nuts and seeds to gather."

"Yes, sir," the blue jays whistled, and after the Boss Bird left them to it, Jay could hear the radio frequency clearing back up in his head.

The Boss Bird was right, though, it was time for work. And so, Jay adjusted the knob in his head accordingly, and turned it to a station that provided some good motivating music to work to. As Jay sang along, he took the lead and naturally provided guidance to his friends as they carried out their duties, hunting for nuts and seeds to the beat of their music.

After a hard day's work, Jay was exhausted, and the motivating music began to grow staticky. So he said his farewells and headed home, adjusting the knob in his head to a station with calmer music to hum along to.

The closer he got to home, though, the more the station's frequency faded out. And upon arrival, he was hearing mostly static again.

"Hello, Jay," said Mother Jay upon his arrival back home.

"Hello," said Jay through the static, unable to find a fully clear channel in his head.

"How was work today?" asked Mother Jay.

"It was okay," said Jay.

It wasn't much, but Mother Jay was elated that Jay was able to sing around her again, even if just a little. And the more Jay sang, the clearer the frequency at home would get, though it was still quite staticky.

> > >

The next day, Jay invited his mother to join him for a quick flight around the woods, and Mother Jay obliged. Jay lowered the volume in his head so as to turn down the static, and he enjoyed the natural sounds all around on their flight.

After taking a lap around the woods, Mother Jay headed back for her home tree.

"Will you be coming home soon?" she asked.

Jay turned the volume back up, and he turned the knob to find a channel that wasn't completely static. After which, he shyly replied, "I'll come home later. I'd like to go for another lap around the woods first."

They said their farewells, and Jay flew back into the woods. As he ventured deeper and deeper, the radio frequency cleared up, and it played a pleasant tune that he happily sang along to.

* * *

When Jay next met with Mrs. Owl,

she asked him if he had given her question any thought, and if so, what he had come up with.

He adjusted the knob in his head to find a clearer station, and he offered Mrs. Owl an answer to her question.

"I've spent some time considering your question," said Jay. "I suppose that if my brain were a radio, then it draws upon different frequencies in different scenarios. Sometimes it comes in clear, and I can speak just fine. Other times, it comes through as nothing but static, and as a result it becomes much harder to break through the mental noise and speak. But in those situations, I've had to learn to adjust the frequency in my head to what best comes through."

"That's very insightful," said Mrs. Owl. "And how have things been going for you since you realised this?"

"There's still a lot of static in certain situations, but it's not as bad as it was before," said Jay. "I think the therapy has helped me to get a better signal, though."

"Well that's great," exclaimed Mrs. Owl. "And how are things around your mom?"

"The signal around her is gradually getting clearer," said Jay.

"And how are things going with your OCD?" asked Mrs. Owl.

Jay gave it some thought, then offered an explanation. "It feels like my OCD once had full control over the radio in my head, and it kept me lost in the static. However, lately I've been able to take control back and turn the knob to a clearer station, even if there is still some static that continues to seep through."

"What do you think it would be like if you had full control over the radio?" asked Mrs. Owl. "What if you didn't have any static coming through on any channel?"

"Hmm," Jay wondered. "I'm not sure."

"Well let's work on that next," said

Mrs. Owl.

"Okay," said Jay.

I'm not saying that I'm cured by any means. I'm not. I still deal with OCD in my everyday life. But the symptoms are not nearly as severe as they were in the past, and OCD doesn't control every aspect of my life like it used to. I'm able to work more hours again, as well as enjoy hobbies that my OCD was preventing me from.

One activity in particular that I was able to take up again was writing. Since my recent breakthrough, after years of not writing, I have churned out many stories, some of which I had been holding inside for years, and others which were inspired by my journey of treatment for OCD and other mental health issues. And now, I've had the pleasure of sharing some of those stories, and through the telling urge everyone to not give up when dealing with similar issues in life. After OCD overwhelmed my life, it took me years of hard work to get my life back. And all the time and trial and error was certainly worth it in the end. So just keep in mind that while it's gonna get worse before it gets better, if you stick with it, life does indeed get better.

I would like to thank everyone who directly contributed to the creation of this book, including Christine Celenski, Chrissy Miller, M.H. Smith, and my Uncle Bob and Aunt Laurie.

And I would especially like to thank my mom, without whom this book would not have been possible.

Growing up, Chris Widdop would constantly escape into the fantasy world that was his vivid imagination, where he took part in many adventures. And now, Chris wants nothing more than to share those adventures with the world.